This Coloring Book Belongs to

_____

_____

My

_____

_____

Gave Me This
Coloring Book

GIRLS ARE

$$3x + 2 - 2 = 14 - 2$$
$$3x = 12$$

$$6 = 2(y + 2)$$

$$y = \underline{}$$

$$\frac{3x}{3} = \frac{12}{3}$$
$$x = 4$$

SMART

Girls
are . . . . .

enthusiastic

GIRLS ARE

CREATIVE

GIRLS ARE

RESPONSIBLE

GIRLS * ARE

1st

PROUD

GIRLS ARE

TECH-SAVVY

Girls are
GENEROUS

GIRLS ARE

$3x + 2 - 2 = 14 - 2$

$3x = 12$

$6 = 2(y + 2)$

$y = \_\_\_$

$\dfrac{3x}{3} = \dfrac{12}{3}$

$x = 4$

SMART

GIRLS ARE

CREATIVE

GIRLS ARE

RESPONSIBLE

GIRLS ARE

AMBITIOUS

Girls are

IMAGINATIVE

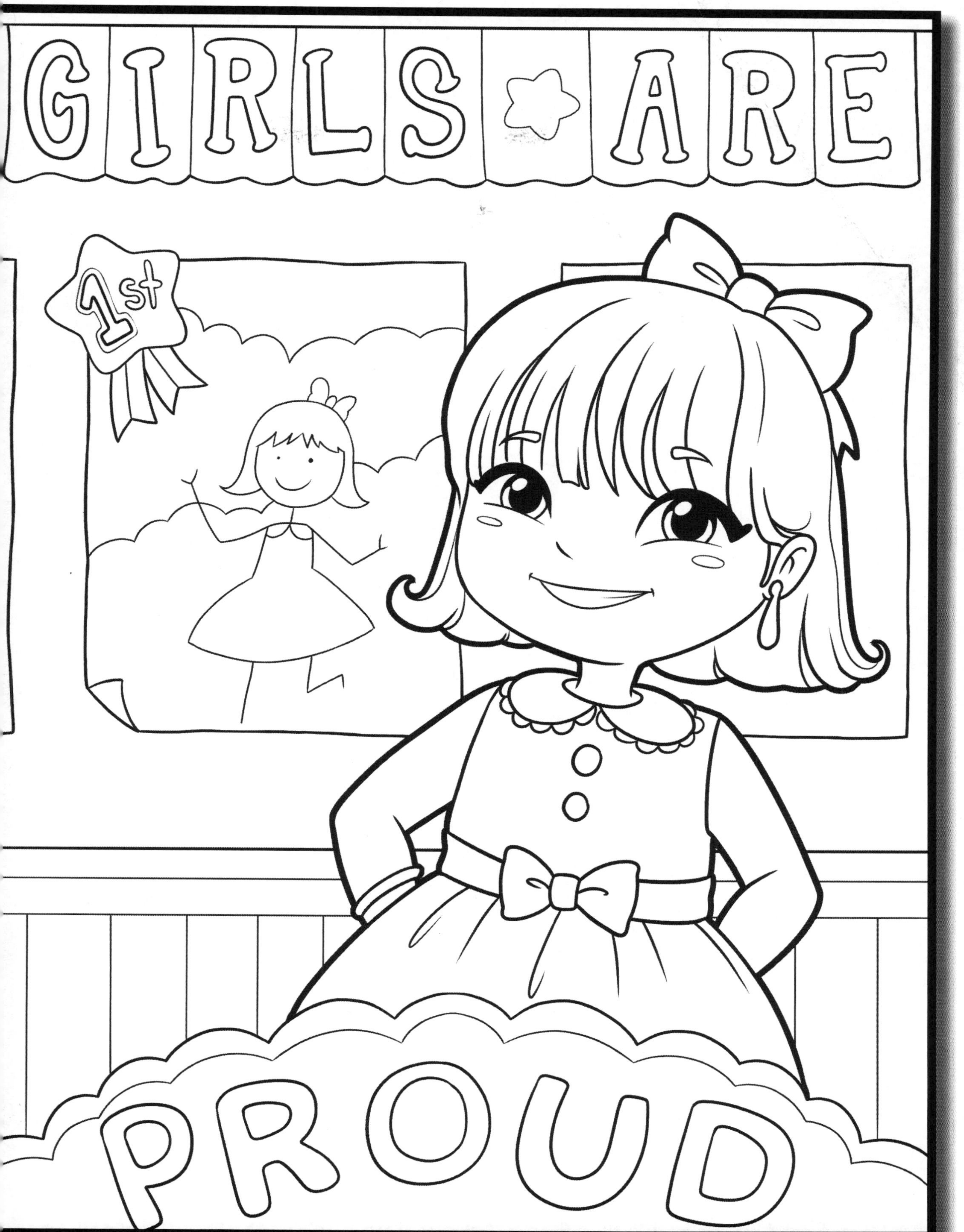
GIRLS ARE
1st
PROUD

GIRLS ARE

TECH-SAVVY

Girls are

GENEROUS

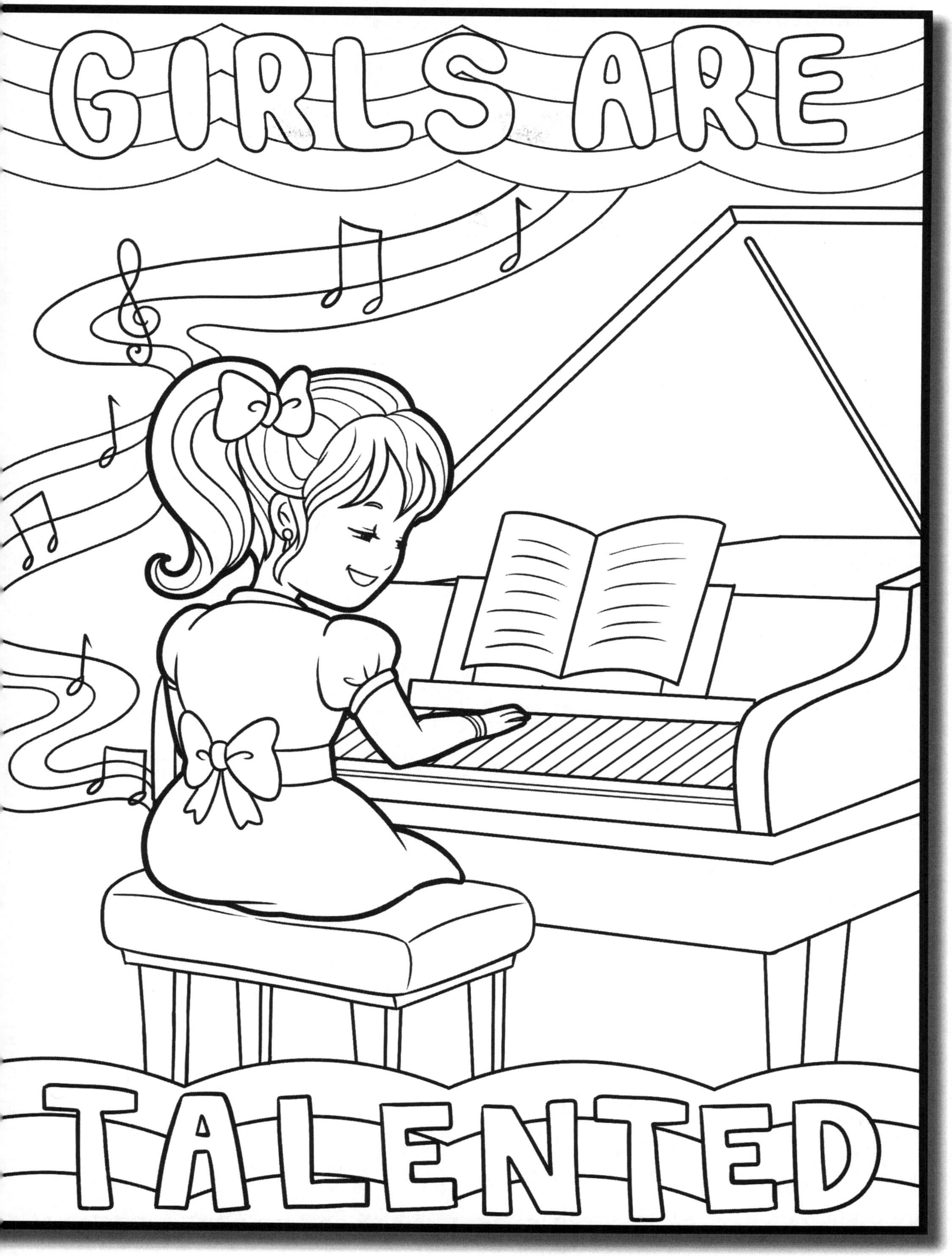
GIRLS ARE
TALENTED

GIRLS ARE ATHLETIC

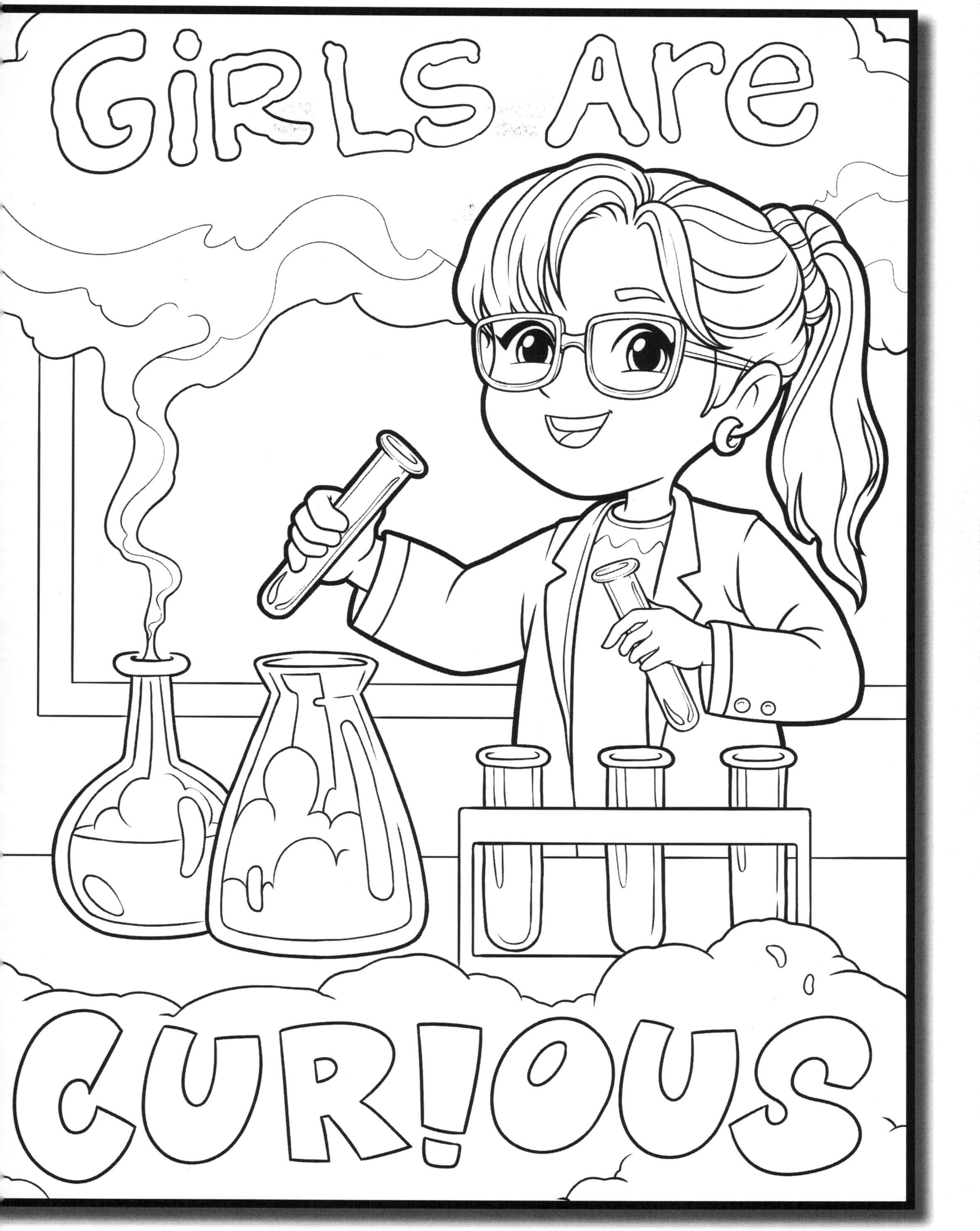
GiRLS ARE
CUR!OUS

Animals for Beginners

Jade Summer

Christmas
Coloring Book for Kids

Jade Summer

Christmas
Coloring Book for Toddlers

Jade Summer

Cute Animals

Jade Summer

EMOJI
50 FUN IMAGES TO COLOR

Jade Summer

Flowers for Beginners

Jade Summer

Mandala
Coloring Book for Kids

Jade Summer

Mandalas for Beginners

Jade Summer

Kids Coloring Book

Unicorns
Jade Summer